For D.A.W.—J.W.

First published in the United States 1996 by
Dial Books for Young Readers
A Division of Penguin Books USA Inc.
375 Hudson Street • New York, New York 10014

Published in Great Britain
by Andersen Press Ltd.
Text copyright © 1996 by Jeanne Willis
Illustrations copyright © 1996 by Tony Ross
All rights reserved • Printed in Italy
First Edition
1 3 5 7 9 10 8 6 4 2

Library of Congress Cataloging in Publication
Data available upon request.

The illustrations are rendered in watercolor.

The Pet Person

Barking by Jeanne Willis
Scratching by Tony Ross

Dial Books for Young Readers — New York

"What do you want for your birthday, Rex?"
"A pet person," said Rex.
"But it'll ruin the furniture," said his mother.

"It won't," said Rex.
"I'll take it for walks."
"We'll see," she said.
Rex went to find his father.

"Can I have a pet person for my birthday?"
asked Rex.

"No," said his father. "It would eat
us out of house and home.
Anyway, they smell."

"Not if you look after them properly," said Rex.

"*I'll* end up looking after it," said his father. "The answer is NO!"

Rex went to see Uncle Fido.

"People make lousy pets," said Uncle Fido. "They can be vicious. What if it attacked your little sister?"

Rex shrugged. "I'll train it not to," he said.

"They are impossible to train," said his Auntie Sheba.

Rex decided to ask his grandfather.
"The trouble with young dogs today,"
growled Granddad, "is that they want it all."
"I don't," said Rex. "All I want is a
person to call my own."

"Why can't you make do with a new bone, like anyone else?" snapped his grandfather. "Horrible things, people."

"Yes," said his grandmother. "They're sweet when they are little, but when they grow up, they develop embarrassing habits."

"Like what?" asked Rex.

"Oh, eating at the table, that sort of thing,"
whispered Grandma.

Talk about giving a person a bad name, thought Rex.

He went to the park, sat at the top of a hill, and sulked.

Down below, dogs were walking their people.
The people were all shapes and sizes. Pedigrees with
fine coats, mongrelly ones, old ones, wide ones, thin ones.

It's not fair, thought Rex. How come those dogs
are allowed to have a pet person, and I'm not?
Then he saw a little ginger one all by itself. It looked lonely.

Poor thing, thought Rex. Maybe it's a stray.
"Here, boy... here, Ginger!" he said, hoping it wouldn't bite.
It came over. It patted Rex on the head.

"There's a good person," said Rex. "Now, sit!"
But the person wanted to play.

It was fun at first. But then it got a bit frisky. It kept on jumping in the mud!

It was noisy.

It frightened the ducks.

It kept wanting to be fed.

And it kept running off and getting into fights.

It followed Rex everywhere.
"Go home, Ginger. I can't keep
you!" said Rex. "Shoo!"
But the naughty person
wouldn't go.

A woman opened
her front door.
She looked at Rex
and frowned.
"Don't play with
that scruffy-looking
thing. He'll give
you *fleas*,"
she said.

"WILL HE?" said Rex,
looking at the boy in horror.
"Thanks for the warning."

Rex ran home—he didn't want fleas. He wasn't even sure he wanted a pet person.

"Guess what we've got for your birthday," said his mother. "I hope it's a tennis ball," sighed Rex.

"No," she said. "But it *is* round and bouncy!"